Thierry Coppée • Story and Art
Lorien • Color

PAPERCUTZ
New York

Thanks again to Valérie for her work behind the scenes.
Thanks to Théo and Julien for the recreational interludes.
Thanks to Lorien for his colors and especially for his kindness.
Thanks to Alma, Cédric, Quentin, and Théo for their lovely hens.
Thanks to Stefano Volza for his tridimensional talents.
Thanks to the Naway offices for their welcome.

To those who like to show off and who know what's lovely.

But especially,
to all the little TOTOS I've met in ten years in school.
Th. C.

To Thierry Joor for trusting in me for the Toto adventure.
To Thierry Coppée who will soon adore pink.
To the darling that I love.
L.

TOTO TROUBLE Graphic Novels Available from Papercutz

Graphic Novel #1
"Back to Crass"

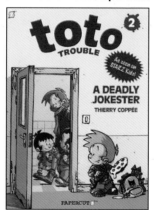

Graphic Novel #2
"A Deadly Jokester

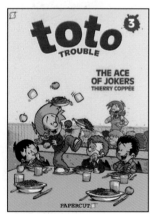

Coming Soon!
Graphic Novel #3
"The Ace of Jokers"

TOTO TROUBLE graphic novels are available for $7.99 in paperback, and $12.99 in hardcover. Available from booksellers everywhere. You can also order online from papercutz.com. Or call 1-800-886-1223, Monday through Friday, 9 – 5 EST. MC, Visa, and AmEx accepted. To order by mail, please add $4.00 for postage and handling for first book ordered, $1.00 for each additional book, and make check payable to NBM Publishing. Send to: Papercutz, 160 Broadway, Suite 700, East Wing, New York, NY 10038.

papercutz.com

TOTO TROUBLE #2 "A Deadly Jokester"
Les Blagues de Toto, volumes 3-4, Coppée
© Éditions Delcourt, 2005-2006

Thierry Coppée – Writer & Artist
Lorien – Colorist
Joe Johnson – Translation
Tom Orzechowski – Lettering
Beth Scorzato – Production Coordinator
Michael Petranek – Editor
Jim Salicrup
Editor-in-Chief

ISBN: 978-1-62991-044-4 paperback edition
ISBN: 978-1-62991-070-3 hardcover edition

Printed in China
September 2014 by New Era Printing LTD
Unit C, 8/F, Worldwide Centre
123 Tung Chau Street, Hong Kong

Papercutz books may be purchased for business or promotional use. For information on bulk purchases please contact Macmillan Corporate and Premium Sales Department at (800) 221-7945 x5442.

Distributed by Macmillan
First Papercutz Printing

"A Poor Example"

SEPTEMBER 3rd...

AGENDA
- Reading
- Math
- Vacation memories
- Reports

BEFORE YOU TURN IN YOUR REPORTS, WHO WOULD LIKE TO TELL US ABOUT WHAT THEY WROTE ABOUT? WHAT DID YOU DO ON YOUR SUMMER VACATION?

WHO'LL GO FIRST? OLIVE?

I WENT TO THE BEACH AND TO MY GRANDMA'S HOUSE, MISS JOLIBOIS. I FOUND LOTS OF CRABS IN THE ROCKS.

THAT MUST HAVE BEEN FUN!

AND YOU, YASSINE, DO YOU WANT TO TELL US SOMETHING?

I WENT TO MY COUSINS' HOUSE IN MOROCCO! THEN I CAME HOME AND PLAYED IN THE PARK!

YOU CAN HAVE A NICE VACATION AT HOME, TOO!

DID YOU GO ANYWHERE, IGOR?

MY FAMILY AND I WENT TO VISIT THE CAVES DOWN SOUTH! WE WERE ABLE TO ADMIRE THE PREHISTORIC CAVE PAINTINGS.

THAT'S VERY NICE, IGOR! AND WHAT DID YOU DO DURING SUMMER VACATION, TOTO?

OH, NOTHING SPECIAL! THAT IS, NOTHING WORTH WRITING ABOUT, MA'AM.

"You, He, She, or What About Me"

BEFORE DOING THE WORKBOOK EXERCISES, YOU WILL NEED TO CONJUGATE THE VERB "TO SING" IN THE PRESENT INDICATIVE!

singular   plural
1) I   1) we
2) you   2) you (all)
3) he   3) they
   she
   it

FOR EXAMPLE, WHAT WOULD YOU SAY WHEN YOU ALL SING?

YOUR TURN, OLIVE!

"WE" SING!

AND YOU, TOTO, WHAT WOULD YOU SAY WHEN IT'S YOU SINGING?

WELL, "I" SING, MISS JOLIBOIS!

AND IF IT'S YOUR SISTER SINGING, YOU'D SAY...

STOPPPPP!

"A Third Helping?"

"*Excused Absence*"

FASTER!
⇒HMMPF!⇐
FASTER!
⇒HMMPF!⇐

WHEW, FINALLY!
⇒HMMPF!⇐
⇒HMMPF!⇐

MISTER TOTO!

SCREEEEECH

?

WHAT EXCUSE WILL YOU MAKE UP THIS TIME FOR BEING LATE?

I DREAMT OF A BASKETBALL GAME, MRS. BLANQUETTE.

DREAMT OF A GAME! AND HOW DOES THAT GAME JUSTIFY YOUR BEING LATE, HMM?

UH, AT THE END OF THE GAME, THEY WERE TIED, SO THEY WENT INTO OVERTIME!

WE PICKED OUT THE ADVERBS IN THE TEXT. NOW I'LL ASK YOU TO GIVE ME SOME SENTENCES USING THE ADVERB "YET."

WHO WANTS TO START?

ME, MISS JOLIBOIS! YESTERDAY, I ATE BROCCOLI, YET IT WASN'T GOOD.

GOOD JOB! I DIDN'T LIKE BROCCOLI EITHER WHEN I WAS LITTLE. BUT YOUR TASTES CHANGE AS YOU GROW UP, YOU'LL SEE!

SOMEONE ELSE?

A CAT CATCHES BIRDS, YET IT DOESN'T FLY.

IN THE FALL, THE TREES LOSE THEIR LEAVES, YET THEY DON'T DIE IN THE WINTER!

I ARGUE WITH MY BROTHER, YET I LOVE HIM!

AND YOU, TOTO, YOU'VE CERTAINLY FOUND YOUR VERY OWN EXAMPLE?

THE EARTH IS ROUND, YET PEOPLE GET IN FIGHTS IN EVERY CORNER!

"Good Day, Goodnight"

TOTO, YOU'VE GOT SCHOOL TOMORROW. IT'S TIME TO GET TO BED!

BUT, DAD, I WANT TO WATCH MORE OF THIS MOVIE!

I REPEAT: "YOU'VE GOT SCHOOL TOMORROW!"

BUT--!

NO BUTS!

ALL RIGHT THEN, I UNDERSTAND!

AND THEY HAVEN'T TAUGHT YOU TO SAY "GOODNIGHT" AT SCHOOL?

WELL, NO, DAD! I ONLY GO THERE DURING THE DAY!

?

OKAY, I HAVE A CHALLENGE FOR YOU, AND IT'S UP TO YOU TO SOLVE IT!

YOU'RE GOING TO FIND WHERE URUGUAY IS LOCATED FOR ME!

PTOOEY

SO, TOTO, HAVE YOU FOUND URUGUAY YET?

I DON'T KNOW WHERE MY AGWAY IS! OLIVE AND CAROL CLEANED THE CLASS DURING RECESS!

"The Truth Hurts"

"One Cousin Equals Two"

DID YOU TELL MISS JOLIBOIS WHY YOU DIDN'T COME IN YESTERDAY?

YES, YES!

DID YOU EXPLAIN TO HER THAT WE WENT OUT OF TOWN TO VISIT YOUR UNCLE AND AUNT WHO'VE JUST HAD TWO BABIES?

I TOLD HER THEY HAD ONLY ONE!

WELL THAT'S RIDICULOUS! WHY DIDN'T YOU TELL HER YOU HAD TWO NEW COUSINS?

'CAUSE I SAVED THE SECOND ONE FOR NEXT WEEK!

"At The Risk of Knowing"

TOTO, TOTO! WAKE UP! IT'S TIME TO GET UP!

NO! I'M NOT GETTING UP TODAY!

BUT, TOTO, YOU HAVE TO GO TO SCHOOL!

I DON'T WANT TO DIE, I'M TOO YOUNG!

TO DIE?

COME ON, LITTLE GUY, GOING TO SCHOOL WON'T KILL YOU.

UH, UH! THAT'S NOT WHAT THEY SAY ON TV!

AND WHAT DID THEY SAY ON TV?

THAT A MAN DIED YESTERDAY BECAUSE HE KNEW TOO MUCH!

"Cyclotherapy"

LISTEN, TOTO! MISS JOLIBOIS ADVISED ME TO GO SEE A DOCTOR WITH YOU.

A DOCTOR? BUT I'M NOT SICK!

I KNOW, TOTO! BUT THIS DOCTOR WILL HELP YOU DO FEWER SILLY THINGS...

...AND YOU'LL DO BETTER WORK.

LATER...

HERE WE ARE!

PHILIP HERKINETICK

CHILD PSYCHOTHERAPY

I'VE LISTENED TO YOU, I'VE TALKED WITH YOUR SON, AND I CAN SEE BUT ONE SOLUTION!

BRAIN OF BOY

WHAT'S THAT, DOCTOR?

BUY HIM A BICYCLE!

A BICYCLE? WHAT AN IDEA! AND YOU'RE SURE HE'LL DO FEWER SILLY THINGS?

OH, NO! BUT HE'LL GO DO THEM FARTHER AWAY!

?

"*Forgery*"

- 23 -

"The Art Critic"

⋛PFFT!⋚ MISS JOLIBOIS REALLY IS THE STUPIDEST SCHOOLTEACHER IN THE WORLD!

?

MY GOODNESS, TOTO, YOU SHOULDN'T SAY THINGS LIKE THAT! AND WHAT'S MORE, I'D BE ASTONISHED IF THAT WERE TRUE!

ANYWAYS, SHE DOESN'T KNOW WHAT A CAR IS!

TOTO, YOU'RE EXAGGERATING!

I'M NOT EXAGGERATING, MOM! WHEN I SHOWED HER THE DRAWING OF THE CAR OF MY DREAMS, SHE ASKED ME WHAT IT WAS!

...

IN ORDER TO SEE IF YOU'VE REALLY UNDERSTOOD THE FUTURE TENSE, TELL ME WHAT YOU'LL DO ONCE YOU'VE FINISHED SCHOOL.

May 15th

yesterday today later tomorrow

I was I am I will be

future

ME! ME!

I'LL PLAY SOCCER!

LATER ON, I'LL BE A LAWYER, MISS JOLIBOIS.

I'LL BE A PROGRAMMER!

AND I'D LIKE TO BE A SCHOOL TEACHER.

AND WHAT WILL TOTO BE ONCE HE'S FINISHED SCHOOL?

?

ONCE SCHOOL'S FINISHED, I'LL BE...

...*CRAZY HAPPY, OF COURSE!*

"Expert Counting"

DADDY, YOU'LL BE PROUD OF ME TODAY!

OKAY, GO AHEAD! SURPRISE ME, SON!

TA-TA-TA-**TAAMMM,** A REPORT CARD WITH A HUNDRED!

WOW! A ONE HUNDRED OUT OF A HUNDRED, CHRISTMAS HAS COME EARLY!

GIVE IT HERE, SO I CAN ADMIRE THAT MARVEL!

⋚**AARRGGH!**⋚ WHERE DID YOU SEE A HUNDRED IN HERE?

BUT, DADDY, CAN'T YOU COUNT ANYMORE? I HAVE A 20 IN MATH, A 40 IN ENGLISH, A 30 IN SCIENCE, AND A 10 IN HISTORY! HOW MUCH DO YOU THINK THAT MAKES?

"*Joking Alone*"

"Tour de Fool"

AND NOW BOMOLAY'S ATTACKING ONCE AGAIN...

...LEAVING THE OTHER BREAKAWAYS BEHIND HIM!

BUT VEVITTE'S ALREADY COUNTERATTACKING, AND CATCHES HIM.

TOO BAD, IT WAS A GOOD EFFORT, BUT BOMOLAY, IT SEEMS, SLEPT VERY BADLY AFTER A BOUT OF INDIGESTION!

HEY, FRANKIE, WHY ARE THEY ALL PEDALING LIKE THAT?

THEY'RE ALL PEDALING LIKE THAT BECAUSE THE ONE IN FIRST PLACE WILL WIN LOTS OF MONEY.

OH!

BUT THEN WHY ARE THE OTHERS PEDALING?

≳SNIF!≲

"I Scream, You Scream, We All..."

- 31 -

"Idiots and Jokes"

SEPTEMBER 4TH...

HERE COMES IGOR. JUST LISTEN AND WE'LL HAVE A GOOD LAUGH!

IGOR, I'VE GOT GOOD NEWS FOR YOU!

?

THERE'S A NEW KID IN MR. LOYAL'S CLASS. HE'S CRAZY ABOUT COMPUTERS! YOU'LL LIKE HIM, I BET.

THINK HIS NAME'S STU... STU PIDGRIN. AIN'T THAT RIGHT, YASSINE?

UH, I THINK SO.

THE BEST THING WOULD BE TO GO ASK MR. LOYAL. HE'S MONITORING THE PLAYGROUND...

SIR, SIR, IS IT TRUE YOU HAVE A STU PIDGRIN IN CLASS?

?!

SO, IGOR, HOW DO YOU LIKE YOUR NEW BUDDY?

"The Soldier's Return"

TODAY, KIDS, YOU'RE GOING TO RUN! YOUR GOAL: GET TO THE TREE AS FAST AS POSSIBLE AND COME BACK!

BUT SINCE I'M COUNTING ON MAKING YOU INTO FUTURE OLYMPIANS, WE'LL PRACTICE PROPER FORM!

YOU MUST PUT YOURSELF IN THIS POSITION AND, WHEN I BLOW THE WHISTLE, TAKE OFF!

ALWAYS TAKE OFF ON YOUR STRONGER LEG. IT'S ON THE SAME SIDE AS THE HAND YOU WRITE WITH!

WE'LL SEE IF YOU GOT THE MESSAGE!

TOTO THE DWARF, WHICH HAND DO YOU WRITE WITH?

WELL, WITH MY MINE! WHY?

?!

"The Family Game"

TELL YOUR PARENTS "GOODBYE," EVERYONE, AND GET ON THE BUS. LET'S GET OUR FIELD TRIP UNDERWAY!

TOTO, GO SIT BEHIND THE DRIVER. I WANT TO KEEP AN EYE ON YOU DURING THE TRIP!

VAYAGE

WE CAN LEAVE, EVERYONE'S HERE!

LET'S GO THEN!

FARTHER ALONG...

...IF MY FATHER WAS A BULL AND MY MOTHER WAS A COW, I'D BE A CALF. IF MY FATHER WAS A BOAR AND MY MOTHER WAS A SOW, I'D BE A PIGLET...

MUCH FARTHER ALONG AND LATER...

...IF MY FATHER WAS A GANDER AND MY MOTHER WAS A GOOSE, I'D BE A GOSLING. IF MY FATHER WAS A ROOSTER AND MY MOTHER WAS A HEN, I'D BE A CHICK...

EVEN FARTHER ALONG...

...IF MY FATHER WAS A RAM AND MY MOTHER WAS A EWE, I'D BE A LAMB. IF MY FATHER WAS A WOLF AND MY MOTHER WAS A SHE-WOLF, I'D BE A CUB--

AND IF YOUR FATHER WAS A STUPID %$# AND YOUR MOTHER WAS A STUPID %!&@#, WHAT WOULD YOU BE THEN?!

A BUS DRIVER?

"Nature's Gifts"

BY JUMPING ON THE GROUND, THE BLACKBIRD GETS THE EARTHWORM TO COME TO THE SURFACE. THEN, ALL IT HAS TO DO IS EAT THE WORM. WE COULD SAY NATURE KNOWS BEST, COULDN'T WE?

SPLORCH

?

HA HA HA!

DO YOU STILL THINK NATURE KNOWS BEST, MISTER?

WHY OF COURSE! I STILL THINK SO, KID!

OH, YEAH?

JUST THINK WHAT IT WOULD HAVE BEEN LIKE IF COWS HAD WINGS, EH?

?

"Tracks and Traces"

THIS AFTERNOON, CHILDREN, WE'RE GOING TO LOOK FOR TRACKS OUR FRIENDS THE ANIMALS LEFT BEHIND.

LOOK RIGHT HERE! A BEAUTIFUL DEER CROSSED THE ROAD.

AND THERE, SIR?

THOSE ARE TRACKS LEFT BY A WILD SOW AND HER PIGLETS.

MISTER, MISTER! THERE ARE MONSTER TRACKS OVER HERE! COME QUICK!

LOOK, THE BIG TOE'S IN THE MIDDLE OF THE FOOT, AND FOUR SMALLER, FINE ONES ARE LOCATED ON EACH SIDE! IT MUST BE REALLY SCARY!

OH, THIS, KID...

...YOU'RE RIGHT. THAT'S THE REMAINS OF A FROG THAT GOT RUN OVER! REAL MONSTERS, INDEED!

"Mail Bomb"

HERE ARE THE PACKAGES YOUR PARENTS SENT, CHILDREN! YOU SEE, EVEN THOUGH YOU'RE FAR AWAY FROM THEM, THEY HAVEN'T FORGOTTEN YOU!

COOL!

THANK YOU, MISS JOLIBOIS!

THIS ONE'S FOR YOU, YASSINE!

MMM, SOME POP TARTS!

THIS IS FOR YOU, IGOR!

THANK YOU, MISS JOLIBOIS.

SWEET! A MAGNI-FYING GLASS TO LOOK AT INSECTS!

AND THE BIGGEST ONE'S FOR YOU, TOTO!

HEY, A LETTER TO ME WAS ATTACHED TO IT.

I BET IT'S A PORTABLE DVD PLAYER!

"MISS JOLIBOIS, AFTER THE LETTERS SENT BY TOTO, I REALIZED HE'D FORGOTTEN SOMETHING IMPORTANT..."

SILLY ME! IT'S PROBABLY A FOLDING SCOOTER!

"...THE PACKAGE MAY BE HEAVY, BUT I WAS DETERMINED FOR ALL THE RULES TO BE IN IT. THANK YOU FOR PASSING THIS ALONG TO HIM..."

OR MAYBE IT'S AN AWESOME SURVIVAL KNIFE OR A--

DICTIONARY!

WE'RE GOING TO TRY TO OBSERVE TWO FOXES THAT LIVE IN OUR WOODS. TO LURE THEM HERE, I'VE TIED TWO DEAD CHICKENS TO THAT POST OVER THERE. THEY PREFER FRESH MEAT, BUT THE DEAD BIRDS WILL STIMULATE THEIR SENSE OF SMELL.

TO HAVE THE CHANCE TO SEE THEM, WE MUST FOLLOW THREE RULES. FIRST, WE BLEND INTO THE BACKGROUND-- HUH?

DON'T YOU HAVE A LESS CONSPICUOUS JACKET? TAKE THAT OFF RIGHT NOW!

UH!

NEXT, KEEPING STILL IS ALSO VERY IMPORTANT!

?

OH, SORRY!

SMACK

I DIDN'T SEE YOU, MISTER!

AND LASTLY, YOU HAVE TO BE SILENT SO THE ANIMALS WON'T BE AFRAID.

NOW HUSH, AND LET'S WAIT!

TOTO, STOP!

?

UH, I WANTED TO BORROW HIS BINOCULARS TO SEE BETTER... SIR!

NOW, WE HAVE EVERY LIKELIHOOD OF SEEING THE FOXES!

SO, CHILDREN, YOU'LL BE GOING BACK HOME TOMORROW. YOUR TIME IN THE FOREST IS COMING TO AN END.

SO BEFORE I LET YOU LEAVE, I'D LIKE TO FIND OUT WHO AMONG YOU REMEMBERS THE 4 ELEMENTS OF WHICH OUR DEAR OLD MOTHER EARTH IS COMPRISED.

FIRE, SIR! THAT'S EASY, THERE'S ONE RIGHT IN FRONT OF US!

GOOD JOB, KID.

THE SECOND ONE IS AIR. IT'S GOOD TO BREATHE HERE.

OH, YES, BECAUSE IT'S PURE!

THERE'S ALSO THE EARTH WE WALK ON, SIR!

AND YOU, KID? YOU HAVEN'T SAID ANYTHING TONIGHT! SO WHAT'S THE LAST ELEMENT?

UH...

LISTEN, I'LL HELP YOU. THERE'S NOT ANY CLOSE TO US, BUT YOU WASH WITH IT! SO...

HMMM.

SOAP!

"Souvenirs and Forgetfulness"

PACK YOUR BAGS, CHILDREN. THE BUS WILL ARRIVE SOON! LOOK EVERYWHERE SO YOU DON'T FORGET ANYTHING.

I'LL COME GET YOU ONCE HE'S HERE.

SO, LET'S PACK OUR BAGS. FIRST MY COLLECTION OF WOOD WEAPONS I FOUND IN THE FOREST.

NEXT, MY SET OF CRUSHED LIZARDS I COLLECTED ALONG THE STREET.

LET'S NOT FORGET THESE AWESOME STONES I GATHERED IN THE RIVER.

AND LET'S ESPECIALLY NOT LEAVE THESE NEVER BEFORE SEEN ISSUES OF CAPTAIN DIARY I FOUND IN THE TRASH CAN IN TOWN.

SO THERE, MISS JOLIBOIS WILL BE HAPPY. I DIDN'T FORGET ANYTHING!

CHILDREN, THE BUS IS HERE! COME ALONG!... WHAT?

TOTO, YOU HAVEN'T PACKED YOUR BAG YET, MY GOODNESS!

"Fabulous Fabulations"

MISTER TOTO, DO YOU THINK NOBODY CAN SEE YOU?

WE WERE JUST KIDDING AROUND A LITTLE, MRS. PECHETON!

FIRST, WHENEVER YOU TALK TO ME, I'D LIKE FOR YOU TO CALL ME "PRINCIPAL." NEXT, I ADVISE YOU TO STOP MONKEYING AROUND!

BECAUSE, WHEN I WAS LITTLE, MY PARENTS TOLD ME IF I KEPT MAKING FACES, MY FACE WOULD FREEZE LIKE THAT FOREVER!

WELL, MRS. PRINCIPAL, YOU CAN'T SAY YOU WEREN'T WARNED!

≈SIGH≈

"Punctuated Explanation"

"Snow Falls"

MISS JOLIBOIS!

WHAT'S GOT YOU CARRYING ON LIKE THAT, ARNOLD?

LOOK OUTSIDE, IT'S SNOWING!

CAN WE MAKE SNOWBALLS, MISS JOLIBOIS?

⋛PFFT!⋚ FORGET IT, MRS. BLANQUETTE'S ALREADY SWEEPING THE PLAYGROUND.

BUT WHO AMONG YOU CAN EXPLAIN WHERE SNOW COMES FROM?

ME, MA'AM! IT COMES FROM MY GRANNY'S LEGS!

WHAT? TOTO, YOU'RE MOUTHING OFF AT ME, MY GOODNESS!

NOT AT ALL, MISS JOLIBOIS! GRANNY ALWAYS SAYS WHENEVER IT SNOWS: "I'D BEEN FEELING THAT IN MY LEGS FOR TEN DAYS!"

"Taste Tests"

OKAY, SOME OF YOU HAVE BROUGHT A BOX INSIDE OF WHICH THEY'VE HIDDEN SOME FRUIT, JUST AS I ASKED YOU TO DO.

THIS LITTLE GAME WILL LET US DEVELOP OUR SENSE OF TASTE.

WHO WANTS TO START? TOTO? HOW ABOUT YOU?

GO AHEAD, CAROL, HAVE SOME! SERVE YOURSELF FROM TOTO'S BOX FIRST.

HAS EVERYONE HAD A TASTE?

WHO'S FIGURED OUT WHICH FRUIT'S HIDDEN IN THE BOX?

IGOR?

THEY'RE REALLY OLD RAISINS!

IS THAT IT, TOTO?

YES, YES.

WELL, YOU CAN BRING IN RAISINS WHENEVER YOU LIKE.

I'LL HAVE TO WAIT TILL WE CLEAN THE RABBIT CAGE AGAIN!

"Zeroes Across the Board"

OH, MY, YOUR GRADES ARE REALLY AWFUL.

LOOK AT THIS-- A ZERO OUT OF 20 ON YOUR MATH TEST.

AND LET'S FORGET YOUR SPELLING TEST FROM YESTERDAY: ZERO OUT OF 10.

AND EVEN A ZERO OUT OF A *100* ON VERBS!

YOUR GRADES ARE WORSE THAN BEFORE. THEY'VE NEVER BEEN SO BAD!

IT'S HIGH TIME WE DID SOMETHING ABOUT IT, SON!

I'LL GO SEE YOUR SCHOOLTEACHER TOMORROW.

MA'AM, I'D LIKE TO KNOW WHY TOTO HAS NOTHING BUT ZEROES ON ALL HIS TESTS?

BECAUSE GRADES LOWER THAN THAT DON'T EXIST!

"Angel or Demon?"

"A Naughty Story"

SO THE FIRST LITTLE PIG LEFT TO GO BUILD HIS HOUSE...

...ON THE WAY, HE MET A MAN LABORIOUSLY PUSHING A WHEEL-BARROW FULL OF STRAW.

THE PIG APPROACHED THE MAN AND SAID:

"EXCUSE ME, MY GOOD FELLOW, COULD I HAVE YOUR STRAW TO BUILD MY HOUSE?"

AND, CHILDREN, WHAT DO YOU THINK WAS THE PEASANT'S RESPONSE?

I KNOW, I KNOW!

AH, YES, TOTO, AND WHAT DO YOU THINK HE SAID?

"HOLY SHNIKIES, THAT'S A TALKING A PIG!"

"It's All in Your Head"

"The Day for Problems"

EXCUSE ME, MISS JOLIBOIS, BUT WHAT DAY IS TODAY?

JUNE 13TH, BUT THE DATE ISN'T THE MOST IMPORTANT THING. I'M MORE INTERESTED IN THE ANSWERS YOU'LL WRITE FOR ME!

RIGHT, WELL, AT LEAST I WASN'T LEAVING EVERYTHING ON MY PAPER BLANK!

"Good Parents and Bad Grades"

DADDY, I'M HOME FROM SCHOOL!

HEY, KID, COME HERE! ISN'T IT REPORT CARD DAY?

MAYBE YOU THOUGHT I'D FORGET IT WAS TODAY, HMM?

LET'S SEE... AN "F" IN MATH, AN "F" IN READING, AN "F" IN PARTICIPATION, AND AN "F" IN SOCIAL STUDIES.

IN MY OPINION, YOU'D HAVE GOTTEN AN "A" IN KNOWING NOTHING!

HEE HEE!

OKAY, TOTO, THIS REPORT CARD IS FRIGHTENINGLY BAD. I WONDER WHAT IGOR'S PARENTS WOULD SAY, IF HE WERE TO COME HOME FROM SCHOOL WITH SUCH RESULTS?

OH, THAT'S NOT LIKELY! HIS PARENTS ARE SMART!

HEY, KID.
WHAT
CAN I
DO FOR
YOU?

MY MOMMY SENT
ME TO BUY A
CHICKEN!

WELL, I HAVE A NICE JERSEY GIANT
CHICKEN, A REAL RHODE ISLAND
ROOSTER, AND EVEN AN AMERICAN
GAME HEN! WHICH ONE DO YOU WANT?

YOU KNOW, SIR,
WE WANT TO EAT
IT, NOT TALK
TO IT!

"Generous Idea"

FRANKIE, FRANKIE! DO YOU HAVE TWO DOLLARS?

?

I PROBABLY DO. BUT WHAT'S IT FOR?

TO GIVE TO A POOR MAN!

HMM, IT'S GOOD TO WANT TO GIVE MONEY TO THOSE LESS FORTUNATE THAN YOU. YOU SHOULD BE PROUD OF YOURSELF, KID!

YOU'RE WELCOME, TOTO! SO WHERE IS THAT GUY?

OVER THERE, IN THE STREET, IN THE ICE CREAM TRUCK!

⇒PFFT!⇐

WATCH OUT FOR PAPERCUT Z ™

Welcome to the snarky, somewhat-stupid second TOTO TROUBLE graphic novel by Thierry Coppée from Papercutz, that itty-bitty company that's dedicated to publishing great graphic novels for all ages. I'm Jim Salicrup, your bleary-eyed Editor-in-Chief who, like Papercutz, knows where the boys (and one girl) are…

They say boys will be boys, and we at Papercutz have published a lot of comics to back that up! It didn't all begin with *Bart Simpson* and *Calvin* (from *Calvin and Hobbes*), or even *Bazooka Joe*. There have been tales of bad boys for as long as tales have been told. Perhaps one of the greatest novels ever written about a boy's life has to be *The Adventures of Tom Sawyer* by Mark Twain. We like it so much we've published two different comics adaptations—one in manga-style by Jean David Morvan, Frederique Voulyze, and Severine Lefevre in CLASSICS ILLUSTRATED DELUXE #4 and one adapted by the great American comics artist Mike Ploog in CLASSICS ILLUSTRATED #19. Both versions are great at capturing the spirit of those two adventurous boys, Tom Sawyer and Huckleberry Finn. Yeah, we know they may force you to read the prose novel in school, but despite that, it actually is a great story.

Speaking of adventure, Papercutz also publishes BENNY BREAKIRON, the story of a French boy who is super-strong, except when he gets a cold. Benny is written and drawn by the creator of THE SMURFS, yet his adventures couldn't be more action-packed. That doesn't mean Benny is like every other super-hero. He's very much a good little boy, yet there are a few mysteries surrounding him—such as where are his parents? How did he get so strong? And why does he hang around with an old cab driver? This is definitely a series worth checking out! (Literally, if they have it at the library!)

Oddly enough, the most believable graphic novel bad boy series published by Papercutz is about a boy who just happens to be a blue donkey, and his best friend is a pig, and he's hopelessly in love with a cow. Yes, I'm talking about ARIOL by Emmanuel Guibert and Marc Boutavant. Each volume features a collection of ten-page stories that cover every aspect of Ariol's life—at school, at home, on vacation, etc. Ariol is just a donkey like you or me—he even loves comics, especially *Thunder Horse*. I must warn you, once you pick up one ARIOL graphic novel, and enter Ariol's world, you'll love it so much that you're going to want to collect them all!

Finally, there's ERNEST & REBECCA, the graphic novel series by Guillaume Bianco and Antonello Dalena. Ernest isn't a boy, he's a microbe, actually, and Rebecca is a little six-and-a-half year old girl. So, why am I mentioning them when writing about bad boys? Because in her own way she may be the baddest one of all. When offered membership in the "Buddy Trio" club, which consists of tomboy Chris, and boys Diego and Ronald, Rebecca sails through the initiation challenges quite effortlessly! Life, on the other hand, may present bigger challenges--her parents are breaking up, her older sister ignores her, and she's sick a lot. But Rebecca is so full of life there's never a dull moment. And the writing and artwork are so wonderful, you'll want to savor every page.

Which brings us back to TOTO TROUBLE. At first glance this series may appear to be nothing more than dumb jokes—and there's nothing wrong with that. But if you look a little closer, you may find that there's more to TOTO TROUBLE than meets the eyes (No, they're NOT Transformers). Being overly literal myself, I totally relate to many of Toto's comic misunderstandings.

And, I'll admit it—I love dumb jokes! I hope you do too! Especially since there's even more TOTO TROUBLE to come! Coming soon: #3 "The Ace of Jokers." You don't want to miss that bad boy!

Thanks,

Jim

STAY IN TOUCH!

EMAIL: salicrup@papercutz.com
WEB: papercutz.com
TWITTER: @papercutzgn
FACEBOOK: PAPERCUTZGRAPHICNOVELS
MAIL: Papercutz, 160 Broadway, Suite 700, East Wing, New York, NY 10038

More Great Graphic Novels from PAPERCUTZ™

DINOSAURS #3
"Jurassic Smarts"
Science facts combined with Dino-humor!

ERNEST & REBECCA #5
"The School of Nonsense"
A 6 ½ year old girl and her micro-bial buddy against the world!

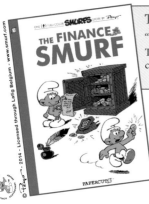

THE GARFIELD SHOW #3
"Long Lost Lyman"
As seen on the Cartoon Network!

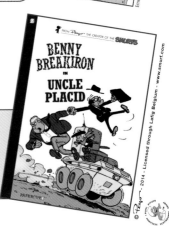

BENNY BREAKIRON #4
"Uncle Placid"
Benny helps his Uncle protect the finance minister of Fürengrootsbadenschtein from all kinds of dangerous danger!

THE SMURFS #18
"The Finance Smurf"
The Smurfs learn that with money comes problems!

LEGO® NINJAGO #9
"Night of the Nindroids"
Will Zane betray his friends? Plus, an all-new Green Ninja Story!